DEIRDRE OF THE SORROWS

PRAISE FOR KENNETH STEVEN

Glen Lyon (2013)

'Robustly and sensitively explores the debilitating consequences of
abuse, violence and the lack of love. It promises even
greater things to follow'

SCOTLAND ON SUNDAY

'This is no ordinary love story but a complex tale of two people feeling
their way towards each other [...] wonderful descriptions of a landscape
and weather unique to Scotland'

SCOTTISH HOME AND COUNTRY

Evensong (2011)

'This collection of poems by Kenneth Steven is stunning. There is a
grave beauty in these lines, revealing a poetic voice of great
sensitivity. These poems are, quite simply, wonderful'

ALEXANDER McCALL SMITH

'For those of us who know Scotland, though not as natives, and for
those of us who are forever attempting to know ourselves, Kenneth
Steven is another inner voice, and never more so than in this collection
of his work. *Evensong* is intimate and beautiful'

RONALD BLYTHE

The Ice and Other Stories (2010)
'Beautiful, enchanting, heartbreaking'

CHRIS DOLAN

'*The Ice* is an atmospheric, wintry tale of fragile human relationships set
in a beautiful but unforgiving landscape'

JAMES ROBERTSON

'*The Ice* comes straight out of a tradition running through Neil Gunn
and Robin Jenkins – precise, sweetly written, slow moving
and with a melancholy air in an uncontrived style'

DES DILLON

'A wonderful short-story writer – a very beautiful, enjoyable collection
from a multi-talented writer'

OSPREY JOURNAL

DEIRDRE OF THE SORROWS

KENNETH STEVEN

This edition first published in paperback in Great Britain in 2017
by Polygon, an imprint of Birlinn Ltd
West Newington House
10 Newington Road
Edinburgh EH9 1QS

www.polygonbooks.co.uk

ISBN: 978 1 84967 388 8
eBook ISBN: 978 0 85790 886 5

British Library Cataloguing-in-Publication Data
A catalogue record for this book is available on request
from the British Library.

Designed and typeset in Dante by Polygon, Edinburgh
Printed and bound by TJ International, Padstow, Cornwall

For Kristina,
with all my love

PREFACE

When I first came to the idea of creating a sequence of poems telling the story behind *A Song among the Stones* (also published by Polygon), it felt something of a breakthrough. For years I had composed the kind of short lyric bursts that make up the vast majority of contemporary poetry collections. It felt exciting to tell a longer story in this new way, offering a miscellany of tiny windows of light into what might have been.

And so it felt right to use this form again when I began to think of a re-telling of the legend of Deirdre and Naoise (the Irish Gaelic pronounced *Ny-sha*). This was a tale I had grown up with: at the close of every family ceilidh, around the open fire my mother would sing 'Deirdre's Farewell to Scotland', supposed to be Scotland's oldest song. A synthesis of sound and sense, it was so hauntingly beautiful – as was the story that lay behind it – that I cried every time I heard it. I learned and remembered the bones of the legend at a very young age.

It's only in recent years I returned to my memories of it and wondered if the fragments of the tale might be shaped into some-thing longer and filled out by the imagination. I also began to think once more of the Deirdre story because I had left Highland Perthshire where I grew up to live in Argyll, and not far from Glen Etive, where the whisperings of legend have Deirdre and Naoise settling. So it was with the western edges of Argyll all around me that I began to re-imagine the legend. But I also felt drawn to work with precisely this story because it felt neglected and even overlooked by artists of all kinds on both sides of the Irish Sea – for of all the great tales of the Celts, this is the great love story shared by Scotland and Ireland. The legend of Deirdre is well enough known in Ireland, though it has been all but forgotten in Scotland.

I wanted the sequence to bring alive the love story at the heart of the legend, to attempt to breathe into it a timelessness and a living strength. For it is old indeed. The roots of Deirdre and Naoise may be as deep as the Iron Age, and it may be – as so often – that some real kernel of truth lies at the very heart.

DEIRDRE OF THE SORROWS

A bird came to her window sometimes
and she wished she might unhinge the slit of glass
to let him in. An eye watched her
as she set her chin on her hands
and watched him back. Most likely he wanted the fragments
     of her bread;
the bird vanished into the green garment of the woods for ever
when she gave him nothing. And then she waited
for sun to tip the branches, and the full light
to set on fire the chamber that was hers.
A girl with a twisted mouth and half a hand
brought food and water with her frightened eyes
each dawn, each dusk. Otherwise she spoke with silence
     all day long
and only watched the woods for shrieks of jays.
At night when the world froze
and the skies danced with a thousand bits of dust
she felt like a child, home awakening in her heart,
and heard her mother calling uselessly across the miles
her name; the sadness of her name.

One night of lashing rain, geese scraggling the low skies
and all the trees gone wild –
Naoise dared to follow for a drink.
The door closed on the dark and he saw
feet following the tunes, faces lit with spilled coins;
his ears hurt with shouted laughter.
He slipped in among them and swallowed beer too fast,
till the world swam and his mouth grew big,
stories appearing as though from nowhere.
It was then Niall spoke of her, as slowly they turned to listen –
a girl kept in the old tower in the forest, like a calf –
pure and perfect, just for the high king –
wide face, blue eyes, all shining.
Niall looked about him, lurched on his stool
as they listened, careful now and watching;
his face spoiled and blotched,
one tooth gone from a fight with Fergus.
He held them all the same, as a fox
watches a rabbit till it's his.
It was Naoise he settled on at last:
And if you try and steal her, boy –
he'll have your blood for breakfast!

Even the trees have ears. His brother had taught him that.
A deer ghosted away on moss hooves;
fragments of rain glittered the leaves,
made of the wood a many-greened goblet.
Naoise knew silence. Once upon a time
he'd hidden from a father dark with drink,
learned how to make trees and rocks
his friends. He crouched now like a moss boulder
and the white tower rose, round, three windows high.
He waited until prickles of pins and needles
crept into ankles and hands. He waited, watching
till he saw her a first time. The wide, white face;
the red-gold rope of hair. His heart filled
and he crouched there yet, so his hands hurt
and he had to move. She saw him;
their eyes met, their gaze held a long moment,
then she turned and the glass was empty.
He waited and hoped and watched
until the rain whispered louder than ever
and he was soaked to the very skin.

All that winter he met her, through the slit of glass.
She watched for him; her smile glowed his heart.
He brought her things:
to admire, to puzzle over, to laugh at –
always her eyes on the trees, for even the trees have ears.
Sometimes her left hand brushed him away;
the high king's men might be watching, for she knew for
  sure they did.
But sometimes there was no fear at all
and he made faces and mimed so she laughed
till the tears coursed down her cheeks.
And when he had slid back into the trees and was gone
she turned over the memory of him in her mind
like a faceted stone, blue and white,
and she thought of him through the long, dark.

One morning before dawn he chanced on her –
the girl with the twisted mouth –
and her eyes grew huge with fear.
He hushed her, held her soft to the ground,
put a finger against his lips.
He had seen her often enough in the tower,
knew what they paid her to do.
Now his words toppled in nonsense,
like boulders careering a hillside.
What was he to do? Could she help him?
What could he give her? How much would she want?
But she stilled him, put a hand on his arm,
whispered that she knew who he was;
understood and wished him no ill.
Her words came in difficult shapes,
so sore and slow and strange.
She wanted nothing, just the promise he'd leave in the tower
a letter saying he was the thief;
for in three days the high king was to take her –
and Deirdre would be his wife.
Now, the girl told him, *you must fly:*
come back tomorrow at midnight!

Naoise fled through the wood till he broke
out into the gold of the dawn,
drank from the chattering stream
till the water had slaked his thirst.
Deirdre, he thought. *Deirdre*.
He whispered her name to the silence
and thought how she now might be his;
she was so close he almost could touch her.

It was the monks who wrote him the letter.
He bought their silence with the few gold coins
left to him, long ago, by his father.
The day breathless and beautiful;
the last gold of the leaves in the birches.

He thought of the way they would run;
readied a boat on its side at the place
where the river opened out to the sea.
All that night he lay hearing his heart;
wondered and worried, wondered and worried,
until light crept into his cell
and a robin sang the dawn.

He staggered naked to the well and broke its film of ice,
gasped at the shock of cold and looked up at the crows
rising like smoke from the woods.
Was all of this madness? What if the girl with
    the twisted mouth
had the high king's men all ready?
He hurt with the fear of it a moment, then blinked.
All he could do was believe; no battle was ever won
without a deep breath of faith. If he failed,
he dared not think of the high king's vengeance.
If he kept a single candle of faith alive –
she might be his, despite all the darkest odds.

Midnight. He could carry no light
for fear the woods still watched.
He knew his way blindfolded; a splintered moon
came and went through gusting skies.
Midnight. His heart drummed
so loud he dreaded it might rouse them.
And there the tower, three windows dark –
for a moment he feared it all nonsense,
that Deirdre slept and the girl had done nothing
but sell him for dirty silver.
He breathed till his fear subsided
and the world stopped spinning at last.
He bit his lip till a single bead of blood appeared.
Then – out of the shadows, across the glade –
as he reached for the door it opened;
the girl with the twisted mouth pulled him upstairs.
Leave the letter here on the table: I'll tell them
you broke your way in and stole her;
the men who watch the woods are at the tavern,
only a handful are left behind,
and the chances are they're asleep. Now go –
take the keys and lock me inside –
throw them away once you have fled!
Only then did he see Deirdre at last,
watched as she and the girl held close,
their faces pressed tight and tender.

Thank you for all you have given;
I'll never forget your kindness.
Then the descent into darkness –
the door thudded shut; the trembling key twisted –
their hands joined as they ran, as they flew,
fast as young hinds, past flickering trees,
further and further till he knew the boat was below them.
Only then did he turn and look, listen –
not a single figure, yet he knew the woods were watching;
he sensed the eyes, felt them burning.
Deirdre tugged at him, dragged him awake and he turned,
hauled out the boat to the water, and it was as though
he feared it might not even float.
But already the land was leaving them
and the thought thrilled through his veins –
it had happened and their eyes met and smiled;
he dropped the keys deep in the water.

And then the sea wove them into her garment;
the slow breathing of the waves, the lift and drag.

What in all the wonder of heaven had she thought of
to follow this boy over the water to Alba?
He scarcely knew her name; like all the rest
he had dreamt something in her blue eyes
and thought he had seen her soul.

Then a yellowness in her mouth, a sourness
that rose and fell until she had to lie,
the sky spinning about her. But he was there,
his blanket over her, his hand smoothing her fear,
and words she could not hear soft against her cheek.

She told him how the girl with the twisted mouth
had said she should run away;
that the high king had no kindness in him,
wanted only pretty playthings.

He told her how first he heard of her,
had lain awake a whole night through –
and when he saw her in the tower window
he'd longed for her to look at him.

They were silent as the land was left behind,
and he did not know what more to say
but found her hand in the darkness
and kept it safe a time, warm in his own.

Not an island, just a ghost of rock –
a bare tooth in the gaping mouth of sea.
She wanted to do nothing but lie in the boat;
he tugged her up to a ledge out of the wind's reach,
wrapped her in his own garment, knelt before her;
babbled words she hardly heard.

How he made a fire she never knew;
her teeth chattered and her hands were raw,
so sore she felt they might not move again.
She stared into the poor, thin frailty of the flames,
not knowing what to say, or caring;
only aware of him about her, scrabbling for seaweed –
anything that might keep the fire alight.

The one thing she noticed, as they descended
and for a moment she raised her head –
Alba, her mountains, appearing and disappearing
out of the shadows of the mist.

She crept into the bottom of the boat
and wanted to sleep and could not.
He made her drink water, fresh from the well
and she thought how it had come from Ireland.
She saw her sisters laughing on a hillside,
and her head filled with colours and new light.

All at once she realised that the sea had changed;
she struggled up and looked at the low sun's eye,
glowing through cloud, as they passed a shore
where rocks glinted and there were birds shining,
slowly flapping on ahead and vanishing.

She glanced up and he was watching her;
she felt the tenderness of his eyes, and somehow
the brokenness of her face smiled, and he nodded
glad and exhausted.

There was a creek where a river tumbled
like the scampering of an otter into the sea.
And he said nothing but brought in the boat;
they clambered out and up, and the sun
burned like a silver disc behind the mist.
She called him and he went, waiting for her to speak
and she said nothing but only took his hand.
A place of hazel woods, of hills and dells,
where birds flitted and wove, and the air felt sweet.
This is a little kingdom, she said, and he thought
how someone had been there before them, once upon a time.
He said nothing but he knew for sure.
And she saw it in springtime already,
awakened with blues and golds. It was a place
for a child to run in and discover.
Let's be here, she said. *We've come far enough for safety.*

How many days that cold?
Even the sun dull and dead,
a snowball muffled by the wintering sky.
The last clutches of rowanberries
like drops of blood on branches,
whorled ice on the pool when she broke it for water.
So still she heard the soughing of swan wings
and saw the four of them swim far above.
They held together in the night like wild beasts
in the rough den he'd made from brush and branch.
When the big winds came, it wouldn't stand a chance.

So there was one whole night he worked,
the moon full: not gold but silver now –
no, not silver even, purest white –
close and clear she saw its every crag.
He built with turf and wood, walls
to last the wind, to keep the winter out.
She watched him where she lay and wanted
to touch his hands. The knowledge came from nowhere.
She drifted through a land
somewhere between waking and sleeping,
was swept away in the end
and woke knowing only that he held her.

Always the fire: the fire was the centre of their world –
they fed it like some hungry god, knelt to tend it
day after famished day. He found whole armfuls of heather,

came back triumphant to make a better bed.
They slept that night –
the hurt out of their hands at last.

Let this be Christmas, she said.
He brought her a strong trout
silver-veined, still slippery from the stream,
the last wild apples from a gnarled tree
right out at the end of the creek.

There was someone here before us, he said;
someone who planted that tree.

They never came to find us, she said,
and he saw the blue of her eyes,
knew why he loved her, for he saw
all of her soul in those eyes.
He wanted to tell her they'd come one day
but it was Christmas, and he could not.

Instead he showed her the single star that burned
above them in the bluest skies,
and held around her, burying his face
in the red-gold field of her hair.

He remembered a prayer his grandfather taught him
the first time they went out to fish.
He breathed it now, too shy to say it aloud.

She said: *I come from a place of waterfalls and flowers*
under a high cliff. I lived beside the sea
and was never in a boat my whole life.
I had three sisters and we ran wild every day –
there was a river with an island;
we made a house of turf to hide in.
My father was a fisherman; he was a kind man,
gentle and dark and strong.
When he took me on his knee he called me Dorrie.
One day he went out and never came back;
they found his boat upturned on the beach
three weeks later. My mother went half mad:
she never laughed again,
didn't come with us to pick flowers,
stopped telling stories.
There was too much for her to do:
everything was just too much.
I was the eldest and learned to do all I could,
but when I grew, when I became a woman,
she saw what could be done with me.
She let them take me away. For twelve silver coins.

He said: *I never knew my father.*
Only a man who beat me. I wanted him to die.
I lay awake at night and prayed that he would die.
There was an anger in him like a coiled snake.
My mother loved him all the same:
she fluttered round him like a butterfly

and all he ever did was hurt her.
But there was something. When I grew older
I could see it in him, a wound that wouldn't heal.

I remember once when I was ten or twelve,
he took me to a field a mile or so away
where clans had fought their worst: some feud
for ownership of land or gold. We stood above the place,
looked down and saw however many men
like broken insects on the ground.
And when they tried to move you saw the blood,
the blackness of it coming from their mouths.
But what I can't forget, still see in dreams,
is the darkness in their eyes and how they looked;
they watched us and I felt the pleading of those eyes.
I wanted then to run, and yet it felt as if my feet
were sunk in mire. I looked up at him, wounded,
to ask why he had ever brought me there.
To learn, he said, and turned to go back home.

They sat a time, said nothing –
saw it was growing dark.
And they lay in the house he'd made
and faced one another. Then they took their fingers
to stroke the soft skin
of forehead and temple and cheek.
Their eyes met and held,
tender and generous, good –
as though they touched the sorrow
deep inside the other.
And not a word was spoken
as night fell gently down.

One day the sun woke her –
she slipped outside a time, marvelling at the light.

Where the stream chattered into the sea
an otter was busying itself with a fish.

There was a thatch of birdsong; she held her breath
for the moss voice of a cuckoo.

She thought of her sisters and for a moment
saw them laughing as they ran to find her;

at their back her drowned father,
the soft shyness of his smile.

But there was no one. She sat
and the sun came in butter yellow;

she felt her face warm
for the first time she could remember –

a hundred tributaries shone from melting snow;
and there, the first bowed heads of snowdrops.

And suddenly she realised that she missed him –
she picked one for Naoise, then ran and ran to find him.

He wanted to make a ring for her
swirled of the flickers of gold he found
from the very river floor. All day he laboured
under the falls where the pools were black,
deeper than he was tall. He scooped them
to swivel a bowl of silt; merlin-eyed
his eyes shone for every glimmer.

But by the time the sun had turned to molten gold,
and lay like a warrior's sword along the west,
he had no more than might have made a mouse's wedding band.
Bowed and bedraggled, he came back,
eyes dark and empty.
She met him; her soft hands raised his face.
Her eyes were dancing and he melted in them;
gave her the smile he feared was lost for good.

Do not despair, she said –
the sun will be our wedding ring.

They ran until they were out of themselves,
and beside the silver jewellery of a stream
she brought him down, gentle, and laid him soft
in a field that was the beginning of summer.
Above them, the swallows flitted and swept
in the open acres of blue-white light.
She brought away his belt and opened him
until he lay strong and shy before her;
their eyes met and she looked at him a long time,
not blinking. With the tip of one finger she touched him –
here and here and here. She ran the finger up and round,
fast and slow, watching his face. He searched her,
wanting to touch her, but she would not let him move.
She closed the lids of his eyes and lay close to him,
and the warm flickering of her tongue set him alight,
so he breathed her name and tried to find her.

Then she was above him and he felt her softness,
the flow of the full curve of her and he gasped.
They held together in the meadow, melded and flowing,
hands wild and everywhere, giving and generous –
closer and closer until the night broke under them
and fell and fell.

Then there was nothing but their own breathing,
the red-gold of her head on his breast and the blue night
filled with the rising of the moon.

One day he came back with news
of a white strand that ran for miles.

They sped there and broke out into the sea:
the delicious cool of it, the blue-green deep.

When evening came they trailed back tired,
talking and not talking.

That night there was no night;
the sky held its blue, so light

they could have walked
for miles and miles unguided.

They did not sleep; there was no need –
instead they sat and watched

like children at a window
with all the summer left to play.

The woods rusted;
great gusts of gold and red,
shuddered to sudden dark.

One night he saw the sky flicker –
a single tail of light. Another and then another.
He rocked her awake and slowly
she came back from another land.
He took her hand and without a word they got up,
went down from the red core of the fire
to the place where they first stood –
the hazel wood above the creek.

The land etched still and silver,
a brilliance to the night's edge;
and now they came in hundreds –
flashes of falling stars, some of them so bright
they gasped as their faces shone.

What do they mean? Deirdre asked him.
Is this some kind of warning?
She held in close to him, searching his face for an answer,
but he knew he could not look at her,
and did not dare say no.

Even the trees have ears.
He woke with the words;
sat up and listened, not breathing,
hearing only silence.

He wrapped a cloak about his shoulders,
went out and stood. His breath smoked the air;
the trees white with rime.
Two deer carved from flint,
saw him and scattered.

Show yourselves! he shouted,
and there was nothing but the echo
from the high rock beyond the creek.

Deirdre lay still,
eyes searching.

If you are here to find us – show yourselves!
The air sore with so much sound
till the silence swam back in waves.

And when he had almost turned away,
believing he'd been wrong after all;
the softness of grass stems
and a boy in white who looked at him,
eyes wide, his voice high:

Everything has been forgiven;
you can come home safe.

Only then half a dozen others
rose from their caves of hiding
and stood – watching, waiting.

Everything she did
was a slow saying farewell:

the fire they had kept alive
through the long torment of winter,

hissed now into a pillar of steam,
a black circlet of sticks.

The house he had made with his hands
that now would fall forgotten;

the place where they first made love,
their imprint left in the stems.

I am ready, she said in the end,
her face bewildered with grief.

They slid into the mirrored water;
a moon of cobwebs above.
She found a hiding place in the boat's bow
to hold her soreness alone.

The hills rose high, rusted with late autumn
and behind them, beyond and beyond
they lay curled in the first snow.

Once upon a time
she had sorrowed for her childhood landscape,
when she was sold to the highest bidder
and carried away in a cart.

She did not cry now, only somewhere
in the secret chambers of her heart
as the men laughed stories around her.

Then his hands holding her; his face deep in her hair;
his murmured words at her cheek. She closed her eyes,
for all this land, this Alba, she loved through him –
without him it would not be.

When they landed she was not there –
so lost in sleep he carried her like a child
curled in his arms.

It was nightfall and they came with torches,
with ropes and chains to take them away:
what more had Naoise expected?

A huge man with foul breath
tried to hide his delight and failed –
She would have married the high king;
we will give her a gentle death –
yours will take a long time.

And still she slept and still he cradled her
as they were taken along some dark road
in a cage kept for wild beasts.

Only when she was torn from his arms
did she awaken, frightened, crying his name,
as they were thrown out into blackness
and a key turned in a lock.

I'm here, he whispered
and found her in the darkness.
They touched and held, as once they did
that first time; the tenderness no less.

It's no different now to when I used to hide,
hoping to glimpse you in the tower. He smiled.

He held her. *All of it was worth our journey.*
There is nothing to regret. They cannot take from us
all we have been given, all we have found.

I want to remember your scent, she said,
so when we waken in the next world
I will know you. Softly, they kissed.

She sat up and looked at him:
And there we will have our child,
the one that should have been.

ABOUT THE AUTHOR

Kenneth Steven spent his first years in Helensburgh, but the bulk of his childhood and adolescence was spent in Highland Perthshire. He was born to writing parents, his father was a journalist and his mother a social historian. Kenneth has always been first and foremost a poet; fourteen of his collections have been published over the years, and he has made many poetry-related programmes for BBC Radio. Birlinn published his novel, *Glen Lyon*, in 2013.

A NOTE ON THE TYPE

Deirdre of the Sorrows is set in Dante, a mid-twentieth-century book typeface designed by Giovanni Mardersteig, originally for use by the Officina Bodoni. The original type was cut by Charles Malin. The type is a serif face influenced by the types cut by Francesco Griffo between 1449 and 1516.